ANGELS
CAN LOVE

VICTOR PAUL

Copyright © 2021 by Victor Paul

Follow Victor Paul on Instagram:
instagram.com/victorpauldomain

First paperback edition December 2021

Book Design by Daniela Owergoor
Typeset by Post Pre-press Group

 A catalogue record for this book is available from the National Library of Australia

ISBN 978-0-6450135-9-7 (paperback)
ISBN 978-0-6453748-0-3 (ebook)

PROLOGUE

I didn't want to be an angel anymore. My mind was made up. I'd never had such an intense feeling my whole life. The way Alice made me feel changed everything. I had very little desire to remain as an angel from that point on. Without any earthly garments or angelic clothing on, there I was, underneath the sheets. Alice was the first human to see me in this way.

With Alice fast asleep in my arms, I wondered if this was the very feeling that I'd been longing for all my life. I wanted to spend every single moment from now on with Alice. I felt connected, loved and cared for in a very strange sense. The One had always loved and cared for me, but this felt different. I craved the human touch that Alice gave me; the warmth of holding her against my chest. I loved what it felt like to be human even though I had only experienced it for a day.

The sun was slowly starting to rise, painting the clouds with ribbons of reds and oranges. My time to decide if I was going to continue on as human or return back as an angel was running out. If I woke up and left, I would return as an angel to The One. I would always wonder what it'd be like to wake up on Earth every morning as a human. What it would be like to feel the breeze upon my face and watch the leaves light up in flames of grand colours at the end of autumn. I knew those thoughts would linger within me for the rest of my existence. However, if I did stay, I would give up my entire existence as an angel. I was opening myself to every other human experience that I had seen so far but not yet experienced.

The One had given me the freedom to decide. Whatever my choice was, it would be irreversible. I got out of bed quietly. I slid into my jeans and walked towards the window of Alice's Manhattan city apartment. What an incredible view. The lights from the skyscrapers twinkled in the Hudson River like stars. The sun had risen halfway. I turned to look at Alice sleeping peacefully. My love for Alice had certainly driven me to this point.

The minutes seem to be ticking dangerously fast. If I did not return before full sunrise to The One, I would be completely human. If I did return, I would be an angel forever with only the memories of being a human for a day and, distant, ineffable memories of Alice. A decision had to be made. I knew there was no turning back—to or from either of the worlds I knew.

CHAPTER 1

A month ago

There was a man in the busy streets of Manhattan who had been homeless for quite some time. He relied on the generosity of strangers, whether it was for a coffee or some loose change. New York City was a stampede of bustling people, every one of them just trying to get a little ahead. Yet, sometimes strangers would be kind. Other times, no one would give him a second glance. He slept on any corner he could find comfort. His shoulders were often hunched—he looked weak, drained and defeated. Every inch of his clothes was stained. He finally cried out to The One for help.

I approached this man slowly. He looked up at me with his sorrowful eyes, seated on the dusty ground. *Just another passer-by,* he must have thought. I was hoping to change his life. I said to him softly that if he was willing to follow me, I would get him some new clothes, bring him to a place where he could clean himself up, and finally get him a nice meal of his choice.

He looked at me, unsure of my real intentions. However, his eyes lit up when I said *a meal of his choice.* Most people offered him very little, if they offered him anything at all. I was offering him much more than anyone else that he had come across.

'You're going to do all that and give me a meal of my choice?' he asked, suspiciously.

'Don't worry. I don't want anything from you. It's just something I'm offering you today,' I said to him encouragingly, extending my hand.

'You're doing this to make yourself feel better then?' he said still sitting on the ground, looking into my eyes and ignoring my hand which was hanging midair.

'I'm just here to help you,' I said, waiting for him to grab my hand.

'How do you know what I want?'

'I'm here to help. Accepting it or not is completely up to you.'

The man introduced himself as Matt. He grabbed my hand and lifted himself off the pavement. I saw that Matt eyed the bag I was holding in my other hand.

'I've got some clothes and shoes for you.'

'Whatever it is I can't pay you for any of that stuff. You know that right?' he said defensively.

'I know. But I'm sure you could do with a new set of clothes and shoes. We could head to a local gym where you could freshen up.'

He told me emphatically that he didn't have any money for gym entry, nor the items that I had in the bag. I assured him that he didn't need to pay for anything. He seemed puzzled but agreed to head to a gym.

'I'm only agreeing to all of this 'cause you're promising me any meal of my choice at the end of it,' he said.

'That's right Matt, any meal of your choice. No questions asked.'

'*Any* meal, right?' he repeated.

'Yes, but first, let's get you freshened up. We're not skipping to the meal just yet.' I said, smiling.

I waited outside the gym after paying for Matt's entry. I felt joy seeing some happiness beginning to surface on his face.

Matt exited the gym in his fresh new clothes. He looked like a new man already. He did require a haircut and a shave though. I intentionally walked towards a barbershop and managed to convince him to get a haircut and a shave. Once again, he only agreed if I paid. I agreed with a warm smile.

It was not long before he was seated on a barber chair. I watched as the scissors and blade worked their magic. Matt's face was starting to light up with a broad smile as the barber announced that he was done. As I was paying the barber, Matt was already waiting outside. He seemed emotional as he looked up towards the sky.

'Are you ok?' I asked him.

'It's just that, I haven't seen myself looking like that in a while. It's funny what you get used to,' he said, trying to hide his tears. He looked away down the street, 'Anyways, I'm starving, do I get to eat now?'

'Yes, of course.'

We headed to a nearby cafe. Matt ordered a large burger, large fries, large glass of coke and a large chocolate milkshake. He dug into it fast. Matt appeared to have been homeless for a long time, and it saddened me. He was eating so fast that I had to tell him to slow down.

Matt thanked me for the meal halfway through eating. I could sense he was waiting to ask me more questions, although the meal in front of him was keeping him busy. He eyed me curiously in between eating his burger and alternating between his beverages. I had just one more thing left for him. I think he could sense it as well.

I wanted him to enjoy his meal. I wasn't going to say anything until he had finished completely.

As if pulled by gravity, my eyes found their way to a woman sitting at the counter of the diner.

A warm sensation embraced my angelic being as I was completely mesmerised just by looking at this woman, laughing with the waitress. It was truly love at first sight.

CHAPTER 2

My eyes were locked on this woman. Her beauty was captivating. Her eyes finally caught mine and I became self conscious. I broke my gaze, a little embarrassed. She could see that Matt was with me. Matt, hurriedly digging into his meal, may have given away that I was helping a homeless person. I wondered for a quick moment what she was thinking. I couldn't help but looking in her direction again. This time, she reflected a warm smile at me. I smiled back.

Just at that moment, Matt asked me again why I was doing all of this for him. He had finished his meal and had managed to break the momentary exchange that I had had with the woman across the room. I said to Matt plainly that I was simply doing a good deed.

'A good deed. That's all?'

'Yes, a good deed. We all need a bit of help from time to time.' I said hoping that Matt wouldn't probe me further with questions.

'I can't remember the last time anyone went to this kind of effort for me,' he said with deep sadness.

If only Matt knew he was actually speaking to an angel. I had one final task to do before I left. I wanted him to reach out to a group of people who could help him.

'I'm going to give you a card. It's temporary housing for people who are trying to get back on their feet.'

Matt was silent at first. I wasn't expecting him to understand everything that had happened that day. The kindness and generosity he had received must have overwhelmed him. Matt finally nodded.

'Okay … so what do I do?' he asked.

'You head to this place and reach out to these

people. They can help you with temporary housing and many other things. What you choose to do from here is really up to you, Matt,' I said supportively, tapping him on the shoulder.

'Thank you … I never quite got your name …' he said, realising that he'd never actually asked me my name throughout this entire time.

'It's Mike … you take care of yourself, Matt. All the best, too,' I said with a smile. I got up and prepared to leave the cafe.

I looked around for the enchanting beauty who had been sitting diagonally from us. Unfortunately, she had already left the cafe. She was nowhere to be found. I felt this desperate urge to see her again. I don't know why, I just did.

CHAPTER 3

My eyes scanned the street as I walked away from the cafe. I wished so strongly that they would fall upon her. She had strangely opened an unknown window into my being. I felt good but I wasn't sure if I was supposed to feel this way. I got lost in thought just thinking about her.

In any case, if I did see her again, I wouldn't know what to say. I knew just saying *hi I saw you at the cafe and we smiled earlier* could be awkward. Also, what else did I have to say to her? *Hi, I'm Mike the angel?* She would totally freak out. I wondered who she was and what her life was like. So many questions and thoughts played in my head as I got ready to get back to The One.

'I'm so sorry,' I said, as my shoulder accidentally brushed past a woman.

'That's okay,' she said, as she looked back with a smile, recognising me.

I couldn't believe it. It was the same woman from the cafe. My wish to see her again had come true. I stood there for a moment, lost for words. I watched her wait for those seconds to pass with a smile. I desperately gathered my thoughts, my brain panic-cycling through so many potential opening words.

'It was so kind of you to help that man,' she started.

'How do you know I was helping him?'

'Well, I kind of overheard the both of you talking.'

'Just helping a person out there who really needed it,' I said.

'Alice …' she introduced herself, extending her hand.

'Mike,' I said, smiling back at her.

She told me that my act of kindness intrigued her. She said she wondered why someone would take time out of their day in this city to help another person. I told her it gave me great joy to help people. She told me she worked as a lawyer in Manhattan. She had never come across anyone who took such interest in a homeless person's life.

She seemed interested in meeting me again. She gave me her card with her mobile number on it after I told her I didn't have a mobile phone for now. She was surprised of course. Fortunately, she had to take off due to work commitments and didn't have a chance to ask me any more questions. In any case, I would have struggled to answer.

This kind of interaction was new to me. I couldn't tell her where I worked, where I lived or how to contact me. Despite all of this, my short interaction with Alice had clearly gone in the direction of her wanting to see me again. She left me with that warm smile of hers and the words *you've got my number*.

A storm of thoughts started to brew in my mind. I was processing what had just happened, and what to do next was still a dilemma. I wanted to see her again but I just didn't know how this could all work out. I sat near a fountain, with my hand covering my forehead, thinking about how meeting Alice again could occur just before heading back to The One.

I can't exactly explain what was drawing me to meet her. All I felt were sparks of excitement at the thought of seeing her again, of running into her on the street, of watching her smile at me. I didn't know how I was going to bring it up with The One, but I knew I had to reveal my feelings somehow.

CHAPTER 4

I had been seeing Alice for over a month now. We met frequently at the same cafe at arranged times, often for lunch. I tried to lead her away from inquiring about my history—all of the things I couldn't tell her. I politely requested that she didn't ask questions about my work. I knew this would raise suspicion, but I got the feeling she was intrigued by my mysterious nature. I assured her in due time I would give her more details, mostly once I figured out what those details would be.

I told her for the time being that I did not have a phone but that would change at some point. Alice often couldn't understand this. We had to arrange catch ups in advance. I also never mentioned where I lived. I believed her interest in me could overcome these minor difficulties.

She often hinted she would like us to be more than our cafe catch-ups. I knew my time was running out before Alice demanded more concrete answers. There was only one way this could all work out between me and her. I had to become human.

.....

My face was a mirror of how my heart felt. Powerful bright rays warmed my shoulders. I turned around. There was The One.

'Why are you disheartened, Mike?' The One asked.

'I think I'm feeling something I shouldn't and I'm very confused about the whole situation.'

'Speak to me, Mike. Tell me what's in your heart.'

'I would like to be a human,' I blurted.

'Why is that so? You are not happy being an angel?'

'No, I love being an angel. But I'm in love with a human … Alice. And I don't know how I can be with her as an angel … My feelings for Alice have become so strong that becoming a human is all I can think about … Oh The One, please help my confused being.'

The One stretched out a hand and touched my shoulders. I was so afraid that I had hurt The One by pouring out what was in my heart. The One had always looked after every angel. Had I asked the forbidden? Was my love for a human, wrong? Even in that brief moment, waiting for a response, I felt terrible asking what no angel I knew had ever asked before.

'If that's what your heart desires Mike, it will be granted to you.'

My eyes lit up as I heard those words. I felt overjoyed with the response.

'I can be a human?' I exclaimed.

'Yes. But you do know that once you are a human you can never be an angel again.'

'I do … but, I'm not sure how all of this is going to work out … Is there any way I can exist as a human even for a day before I make up my mind?'

The One paused before answering, 'You are asking something that has not been granted to any angel before. However, I do know the weight of the decision you are faced with. Very well then, you get to be human for a day. If you do not return before full sunrise tomorrow, you will be human forever.'

I was overjoyed to be given the chance to exist as a human for a day. The One reminded me that I was solely responsible for my decision.

Frankly, my heart was so delighted that nothing else mattered more than experiencing being human with Alice for a day. Honestly, I didn't put too much thought into the entire situation. After all, I had till sunrise the next day to decide. I thought that would surely be enough time.

All I had to do was try to get Alice to spend the full day with me. Unbeknownst to her, I had a life changing decision to make.

CHAPTER 5

My first day as a human being was exhilarating. Every breath, every heartbeat, everything I touched, every breeze I felt was bewildering, astounding. I felt alive.

I couldn't wait to meet Alice—to hold her hand as a human, to embrace her as a human. Entirely unknown to her, I would be experiencing all these earthly sensations for the very first time.

On the way to the cafe, I came across an angelic fountain at a quiet spot near a park. These angelic fountains often appeared to me when I was on my way to help someone. I would find in that fountain what I needed to help others. These fountains were only visible to angels. The human eye would not be able to see them.

I walked towards this fountain, puzzled as to why I was able to see it. Did The One intentionally allow me to see this fountain? I found a wallet inside its basin. I picked it up. The wallet had no cards in it, but I did find some money and a note. I opened up the folded note. It read:

Dear Mike,
Just remember, I'll always be there for you.
Love,
The One

An uncontrollable tear fell right off my cheek. I remember playing songs of love and friendship in the cool of the evenings to The One. Those moments would become distant memories if I became human forever. I had been an angel with the gift of music; a talent I truly treasured.

A tinge of discomfort made me reconsider what I was doing. I wasn't even sure if Alice was going to feel as deeply as I did. At this stage, the desire to meet her and express my feelings was over-powering. I couldn't contain them. I reminded myself that my feelings for her were the very reason why I was even human for a day today.

Time seemed to slip away now that I was on a time limit. As I reached the cafe, I looked around impatiently for her. I wished I could see her that instant. She turned up apologising, saying something had come up at work and she could only meet me later in the evening. She promised to make it up to me by buying dinner. She also told me to meet her at her favourite restaurant at five that evening. She left me with a kiss on my lips. I couldn't tell her that I was on a time limit that day and every precious moment with her mattered. I smiled and said that I couldn't wait to see her. It was the first time she had kissed me on the lips. I felt powerful rays of emotions running through my body. This was a whole new experience for me. And there was no one I could share it with but myself and my own thoughts.

I decided to use the time I had to walk around Manhattan. I came across the same spot that I had helped a homeless man almost a month ago. I smiled to myself seeing that spot empty. My mind envisioned various scenarios of me and Alice. I was optimistic that Alice and I could be very happy together.

I didn't know any of the concrete human details, like what I was going to do for work or where I was going to live. That thought concerned me but I was certain I had plenty of time to decide later. I truly believed that Alice and I would be able to overcome any obstacles together.

I had enough money to get a couple of meals and stay in a motel near Manhattan for a few days. But that was it. After that, I knew I would have to work my way through this world and earn enough to survive.

The afternoon light was fading slowly. I had walked around with so many thoughts in my head that it was now time to meet Alice at the restaurant. My palms were drenched with sweat as I saw Alice wave to me across the street. The next few hours would be crucial in determining my final decision.

CHAPTER 6

Alice nervously tucked a piece of hair behind her ear as she approached me. She apologised once again and then threw her arms around me. I felt so warm. It was like she was my missing puzzle piece.

Alice began, 'Sorry about earlier. Work, you know. Dinner's on me.'

'It's okay. I'm just glad you're here now.'

We had a great chat about her job and her family. As for me, I didn't say much. I couldn't tell her anything about my transition at this stage. I didn't want her to flip out.

When asked about my job again, I simply said I didn't want to discuss it tonight. I let her lead the rest of the conversation. Alice continued to speak more about herself. Thankfully, she was doing most of the chatting that night. She was very proud of her family's law firm, owned by her father. She lived in an expensive city apartment in Manhattan that she wanted me to see. We had a few drinks at this stage and I must admit I felt really light-headed. Having been an angel up to this point, this was my first human experience with alcohol.

Alice told me that she didn't normally invite anyone over but she felt that I was someone special. It ignited my heart to hear her say that I was special to her. As we walked hand in hand towards her apartment, she suddenly said, 'You know, you're really solidly built.'

'Yeah, I guess so.'

'I mean, how often do you work out?'

I laughed and said, 'It's just the way I look.'

'Is that right?' she giggled and then squeezed my hand.

Once we were in her apartment, she put on some music and opened a bottle of wine. Halfway through my glass of wine, I felt her warm lips pressed against mine. Before I knew it, I was shirtless. She ran her hands along my body and when I kissed her back, both our passions fired up. It was an unforgettable moment for me.

We made love and fell asleep holding each other tightly. I was now certain Alice felt just as deeply for me as I did for her. The next time my eyes opened, I saw the first rays of sun were slowly creeping through her blinds. I got out of bed quietly so as to not disturb Alice. This could be my last sunrise as a human. I struggled in these final moments.

I turned around momentarily taking my eyes off the rising sun. Alice was curled up under the sheets, so beautifully asleep. All of a sudden, I could see our lives together. I turned back to look at the sun continuing to rise. With seconds from full sunrise, I finally decided that I was going to continue my existence as a human. There was no turning back for me now. I accepted the full consequence of my decision. At that point, the sun had fully risen. I felt a strong powerful heartbeat in my chest. I knew that that was the moment, not only was I human, but human forever.

CHAPTER 7

Alice woke up with a sleepy smile. I was wondering what the next step would be for us. Everything was new to me. This whole thing with me and her, whatever it was. I wanted to stabilise myself before talking about anything to do with my past.

'I had a great time last night,' she started.

'So did I.'

We got chatting and she dropped me a question that I couldn't really answer. She wanted to know where I stayed. Suddenly nervous about where I was going to live after today, I thought it was time to let her know that I didn't have a place to stay at the moment. Of course, this took her by surprise.

'What happened to your place?'

'I don't live there anymore.'

'What do you mean?'

'It's complicated Alice; I just don't live there anymore.'

'Wait a minute Mike … where do you live now?'

'I … um … I …' I stumbled over my words.

'Mike … what's going on? A few weeks ago I saw you help a homeless man get back on his feet and now you can't seem to tell me where you live?'

'Alice, it's hard to explain but I've given up everything in my previous life to be with you.'

'What do you mean you've given up everything to be with me? Who are you, Mike? What is it that you're hiding from me? Is Mike even your real name?'

Alice's eyes stared straight into my soul.

'It's Mike …'

'Mike what …?

'It's … just Mike.'

'Alright, show me your driver's licence,' Alice forcefully demanded.

'I don't have one, Alice.'

'Okay ... well ... I guess you don't need one if you've lived your whole life in Manhattan ... but where have you been living this whole time?'

'Alice, it's complicated. I need some time to sort things out. I'll explain everything soon—'

And then she said it.

'I'm sorry Mike, I can't see you anymore. Your situation is bizarre. I've thought that for some time now but I also thought I'd have answers by now.'

'Alice, I love you,' I blurted out just as she finished her sentence.

'Oh come on, Mike. You've known me for what ... a month? Now you're in love with me?

'Alice, you don't know what I've given up to be with you.'

'What exactly did you give up to be with me, Mike?'

'I left another world to be in yours and—'

'Alright, this is getting ridiculous ... you need to leave now.'

'Wait, Alice, I'm sure we can work this out.'

'Mike, there is no we,' she said pointing firmly to the door, wanting me to leave.

'Alice let me —'

'You need to leave now!' she said forcefully.

There was a moment of uncomfortable silence as I walked towards the door.

'Alice, I love you.' I repeated as I was about to close the door behind me.

'Mike, just stop ... I don't want to see you again. Go!'

I closed the door behind me and exited her apartment, feeling shattered.

CHAPTER 8

That was it. The words that came out of Alice's mouth were stone cold. Alice had no idea what I had sacrificed to give our relationship a chance. Now, I had nowhere to go and very little money on me.

There was no way of convincing Alice. She couldn't see a future with me. She was attracted to Mike the angel. However, Mike the human was not someone she wanted to see anymore, especially after our heated conversation.

I walked along the streets with a heavy heart. I felt like bursting into tears and never stopping those tears. I had made a mistake by coming into this world as a human. I felt heart-broken as I walked aimlessly through the streets of Manhattan. A vast emptiness filled my heart. I was lost and lonely.

I knew Alice was gone. I felt my only chance of changing her mind was to have a place and a job of some kind. I was confused. I didn't know where to start. I was overwhelmed with emotions.

I came across a music store and saw a guitar on display. I had always managed to convey my love and devotion through music when I played for The One. Perhaps I could also express my sorrow through music. I went into the music store and bought the guitar with whatever money I had on me.

I was hurt, blindsided, naive and in love. My days of being an angel had disappeared since sunrise. There was nothing I could do now but simply live with the decision I had made. I took my guitar from its soft case and decided to play at a walkway.

The lyrics of a song were in my head and a tune had already formed. With a heavy heart, I sang to anyone and everyone around me. The music simply flowed. A massive crowd had gathered, watching me sing and perform. I gave it all in that song and ended it by plucking the strings of my guitar. A man in an immaculate grey suit was watching my every move and listening to my song intensely whenever I looked up towards the crowd throughout my performance.

A massive applause exploded across the audience at the end of my song. In that brief moment, I forgot how sad I felt and a weak smile broke out across my face.

'Thank you everyone … thank you,' I said.

The crowd dispersed soon after. The guitar case on the concrete floor was filled with several dollar bills and coins.

As the very last of the crowd dispersed, one man remained. He was the same man who was closely watching me throughout my performance. He walked right up to me and extended his hand.

'Name's Jimmy … I'm an agent for Mountain Summit Records.'

'Oh hi Jimmy … I'm Mike …'

I quickly formulated a surname in my mind.

'Mike D'Angelo.'

'I like your name … it's got a ring to it.'

'Thank you.'

I wondered what this Jimmy guy wanted. I was curious why a man like him would even take note of me. I clearly had nothing to offer him.

'Did you write that song you just played?'

'Yeah I did … why do you ask?'

'Mike that was raw talent. I haven't seen that in a while.'

'Thank you … I used to play for … um … I enjoy playing the guitar and singing.'

'Mike, I'd like you to swing by my office at two today. We can talk further,' said Jimmy, handing me his cream-coloured name card.

'Okay … and what are we going to talk about?'

'You'll need to play that song you just performed … I've got to go, but I'll see you later.'

Just like that, Jimmy took off. I watched as he hurried away on his business amidst the sea of people, disappearing slowly away from my sight. I didn't know what to make of the meeting with Jimmy. He seemed to have seen something in me. Something I wasn't even aware of. I was left confused. Was Jimmy sincere about meeting me again and what could he possibly want from me? All I knew was that I sang a song that clearly impressed not just the crowd but apparently Jimmy as well.

With the loose change and notes I got from my performance, I managed to get myself something to eat and drink. I was starving and hadn't eaten all day. I hadn't even thought about where I was going to stay for the night at this stage.

My thoughts went back to Alice again. She hadn't even given us a chance. Couldn't happiness be found in love itself? Could it be possible that love will find its way and make everything work out so long as you have each other? Apparently, it wasn't so in Alice's world. Maybe I had fallen in love too quickly. Maybe I was gullible. How can someone be in love after knowing the person for only a month was what Alice had told me. Well, it had happened to me. If only she knew. It was love at first sight. Would it have been different if I was a human from the start? Maybe, I wouldn't have fallen so quickly. I didn't know the answers to some of these questions in my head.

I felt an angry flame burning in my chest. It was rage and disgust. Well, if status, money and lifestyle were all that mattered, I'm going to get it all. I had an appointment with Jimmy. I could feel in my heart that something was going to come of it. Maybe I could use my musical talent to make something of myself.

I wasn't sure how I felt about Alice at this point. Mostly confused, but largely broken-hearted that she had left me unloved. Did I still want to be loved and accepted by her? Yes I did. I couldn't deny that. But I was fully aware of where she stood on this matter. I didn't stand a chance at seeing her again. Not now at least. However, making my way to Jimmy's office might be a starting point for me.

CHAPTER 9

I nervously made my way to Jimmy's building. I walked past the concierge. A security guard stopped me as I walked past him.

'Who are you looking for?' asked the security guard firmly.

'I have an appointment with Jimmy and—' I started.

'That's what everyone says.'

'No, I do have an appointment with him and he gave me his card to come by his office at two today.'

The security guard told me to hold on and made a phone call. He ended the call with *not a problem Jimmy, I'll let him know.* He asked me to wait for

Jimmy to come down and get me. I saw Jimmy approach with a smile while I waited nervously. I didn't even know if I was prepared for whatever this meeting was about. I had my guitar and remembered the song I had sung earlier on, just once. I could perform the song again but what else?

'I'm sorry. I should have told you to give me a call when you got here. You can't get into our office without a security card,' said Jimmy, waving his security card.

I smiled, signalling it was okay. I wanted to ask Jimmy all the questions in my head as we got in the elevator heading up to his office.

'Look, Tony can be pretty harsh with his words, but I'm very sure he's gonna love what you've got.'

'Who's Tony … and what do I—'

'Tony is the guy who may or may not give a green light on your career. I'm pretty sure you don't want to be busking all your life,' said Jimmy, as he patted me on my shoulder.

The elevator door opened before I could say anything and we walked into an office full of busy people. Everyone was swarmed with work. A couple of staff members were busy on the phone.

Jimmy knocked on Tony's office door. Jimmy stuck his head around the door and said, "Tony, I've got the guy we talked about." I wondered what Jimmy had said to Tony. The entire day up to this point had been mentally exhausting and I was doing my best to keep up.

'Come in,' Tony called.

We entered an office filled with awards hanging from every wall. Tony looked serious and it felt like every minute I was in his office, I was intruding his privacy.

'Tony, you've got to listen to this song by Mike ...'

'Alright, Mike, fire away ... I've got an important phone call to make in exactly five minutes,' he said as he eyed at his watch.

I hurriedly took out my guitar from its case. I sang and played the song without any delay. I could feel the intensity of Tony's eyes on me. It felt like his gaze alone could burn me up. But I stayed true to my performance and ended it with plucking a few strings of my guitar as before.

Tony leaned back on his chair and folded his arms. I waited for him to say something in those intense moments. Jimmy had a big smile that had already formed before Tony had spoken.

'What do you think?' asked Jimmy.

'Get him a slot at a few of our venues and let me know how things go in the next few months.'

'That's great ... alright Tony, I'll do that right away.'

'Good luck and we need more songs from you, Mike,' said Tony, as he signalled us to leave him alone.

I could see that Jimmy was thrilled. He patted me on the shoulder and said he was going to get me a gig as soon as possible. Here Jimmy was, discussing a gig, contracts and how many songs I should perform, and there I was, with just one song, my guitar and no idea of even where I was going to put up for the night.

'Jimmy, I know this is embarrassing but ... I don't even have a place to stay at the moment. I don't have much money either.'

'What? Okay Mike, okay ... okay ... we'll need to sort your lodging out ... I can get you a rental place from a friend of mine who is managing it. I'll set you up for a month but after that you gotta pay your own way. I'll pay first but once your advance payments come through, I'll deduct accordingly.'

'Jimmy, I don't know what to say?'

'Well don't thank me too soon 'cause the payment I'm making for you will be coming back to me once the money starts coming in from your venues!' said Jimmy.

'Still, thank you.'

'You'll go far with that talent of yours Mike, but you've got to get cracking with writing more songs.'

Just like that, I was introduced to the music scene. I wrote more lyrics and the tunes just followed through. I played all types of songs. Love songs, sad songs, songs of friendship, songs of hope, songs of loneliness and many others. The crowd loved it, whichever venue I played at.

Things in my life improved so much finan-cially. I lived in a nice apartment in just a few months. I had better clothes and material posses-sions of all kinds. Still, I had this lingering sense of sadness. I wished it would go away. Every night, the sadness returned like clock-work. So, I drank every night after my performances.

My apartment in Manhattan was perfect for after-parties as well. I plunged into a life of alcohol. I had a few short-term relationships but nothing came close to feelings of love. The very thing I felt for Alice simply wasn't happening with any of the women I was involved with. Therefore, I drank more. Hoping I could feel the same way again.

One day, when I'd sobered up in the morning, a thought dawned upon me. The money I had made in the last few months, through my live performances, had allowed me to live a lavish lifestyle. I had expensive clothes, shoes and ate some of the best cuisines in New York City. I could now show Alice the man I had become.

I was battling with my thoughts of whether to contact Alice again. During this time, I was drinking on a daily basis to help me cope with the pressure and the stress of my career. I had not run into Alice since she'd told me to leave. A part of me wished I would run into her and maybe strike up a conversation. Then again, I didn't feel I was ready to talk her again, even if I did run into her. I don't know why, but I still felt inadequate, especially for Alice.

I also wasn't the same Mike Alice had met initially. I can't remember the last time I had extended anyone any help. I was so caught up in my own lifestyle that all that mattered to me was myself. The contract I had signed was also keeping me on my toes. I needed to write several new songs in a small time frame and there were so many shows to perform each week. I was heavy into parties and drinks after my performances every night. It wasn't always a party at my apartment. Sometimes I would get invited to someone else's place. During these months, there seemed to be a lingering emptiness. Feeling surrounded by lots of people and hanging out together didn't make any of that emptiness go away. Neither did drinking. But I still gravitated towards those things, hoping they would fill up the void.

One day, after I got back to my apartment, I sat back on my Italian leather couch, completely exhausted. I opened up the most expensive whiskey I had. I drank it straight from the bottle. As the alcohol flooded my blood stream, thoughts of Alice flew into my memory. I still remembered the times we spent together; the way Alice made me feel. I didn't know how I was going to go about contacting her again. Once again, I was lost. I simply finished up the bottle of whiskey.

CHAPTER 10

Months went on. Jimmy desperately tried to get me to pull myself together. He told me I was on a road of destruction and ruining my career. Every show was combined with alcohol and random women for company. It was a repetitive cycle, and I couldn't change any of it. He told me a story of a lead singer that he was previously managing who had gone down my path and was currently in rehab. His words didn't have much effect on me.

One night, Jimmy told me that some prominent people in the industry were going to be at my show. I gave the best performance I could with several new songs that I had written. The crowd went crazy that night. Jimmy said he was really happy and we could surely move things to the next level after that night. I was glad with the outcome, but I couldn't wait to drink at the end of it.

Jimmy left the venue not long after my final song. I sat at the bar on my own and had one drink after the other. A woman approached me. Sarah, as she introduced herself, had a striking resemblance to Alice. I pulled her close and kissed her.

That was about all I remember of that night.

CHAPTER 11

The room felt hot even with the curtains closed. My head felt heavy and I slowly opened my eyes to the morning. I felt soft tender hands across my chest. I turned my head to the right and Sarah, from the night before, was naked under the sheets and fast asleep.

She was breathing softly with strands of her hair spread across her face. I was about to get out of bed to get a glass of water. I gently moved Sarah's hands and got out of the bed. I picked up my boxer shorts from the ground and slid into them. I looked around my apartment. There were empty whiskey bottles and empty beer cans everywhere. What a mess the place was.

My phone screamed. I walked towards my phone which was on my kitchen bench top. It was Jimmy. I was in no state to speak to him. Sarah started to wake up from the sound of the phone.

'It's my agent. I'll need to speak to him …' I said, hoping she would get dressed and leave my apartment. I wasn't in the mood for having anyone around. I wasn't talking much either. Sarah got the point, got dressed and left the apartment.

I felt lonely, down and depressed. After months of alcohol abuse and crazy partying, I felt nothing but regret for all the choices I'd made in my human life. My mind pulled me up on every wrong decision I had made. I opened up a new bottle of whiskey and again, drank it straight from bottle. I wanted to stop the thinking. I passed out holding the empty bottle in my hand and woke up to the wee hours of the next morning. My hands felt shaky. I got up and looked for my phone. There were nineteen missed calls.

I pulled myself together and called Jimmy in the morning once I had sobered up. He was angry that I had not picked up any of his calls. I told him I was having a rough day and apologised. He told me he had good news on his end. Performances of mine were getting sold out and I was going to be on the road for a while performing at different venues throughout the country.

I agreed. I didn't have anywhere else to be or anyone to be with. The road seemed like a better option at that time. Months of tour, parties and more drinks. I was more lost than ever. My drinking got so bad that I had lost a lot of weight. I would hardly eat and my performances were sloppy. I lost some contracts and many booking agents pulled out. Finally, Jimmy suggested I go to rehab and get some help. He even recommended a rehab centre.

Despite all of this, I decided to push on with my remaining shows. I thought maybe I could pull myself together.

CHAPTER 12

I messed it up at almost every venue. Word got around pretty fast and no one wanted to book me for a show. Not until I got my alcohol problem under control. I was angry at myself more than anyone else. I had given up being an angel to become a human, all for a love that never quite existed in my life.

I wish I could turn back time and talk myself out of that painful decision, but my feelings were so strong at that point that I don't think I would have done anything differently. I felt trapped and lost. I didn't have any real friends to talk to. There wasn't a shoulder I could lean on. I was out of my contract and there wouldn't be another one in sight with all the mess I'd created. Jimmy decided he wasn't interested in dealing with me unless I got myself into rehab.

'Look here Mike, I don't have time for this. I've got Tony on my case and this time you've screwed up badly … I've got to let you go. Get yourself into rehab. That's my advice,' he said, as he turned his back and walked off abruptly.

I decided to move out of Manhattan to clear my head. I moved to Brooklyn where I could use the remaining money I had to get sober on my own. I wanted to go back to writing some new songs and set myself on a better path.

I moved into a small apartment. I met Robert, a guy living next door. Robert himself was struggling with alcohol. I guess I just cracked. We ended up drinking together from sunset to sunrise talking about our lives. Days turned in weeks and I lost track of time. Before I knew it, I'd missed a month's rental payment. There was no food in the cupboards. The apartment reeked of alcohol. There were empty beer cans and spirit bottles everywhere. When I ran into the landlord, he told me that if I didn't pay by that afternoon, he would have all my things thrown out.

It turned out, I was wrong about the rent—I was actually behind by two months now and the landlord had had trouble getting hold of me. I went to a nearby ATM to check the balance on my account, hoping I would have enough money to pay my overdue rent and buy myself some food. I was starving. My stomach was in such pain that it felt like it was tied up in all sorts of knots. I took a huge breath and inserted the card into the ATM. I fantasised that after I had entered my pin number a miraculous amount would appear. All that appeared was five dollars and forty nine cents. That's all I had to my name.

'Damn it!' I shouted, slamming my palm hard against the ATM screen. I withdrew my card and headed straight to the nearby liquor store. I found myself the cheapest alcohol I could get my hands on. I headed back to my apartment, grabbed my guitar and placed it inside its case. The landlord barged in.

'So? What's the story Mike?' he boomed with authority.

At this point, I had already drunk half a bottle of port. I couldn't be bothered dealing with the landlord. I had a small backpack, where I shoved some of my clothes. I strapped the bag to my back and slung my guitar across my shoulder. I downed the remaining port and slammed the empty bottle hard against the coffee table.

'I'm done with this place!' I shouted as I walked past the landlord and left the apartment. I walked and walked, stopping whenever I felt my legs couldn't take me any further. I played songs on my guitar and sang whatever lyrics came to mind. I'm not sure how long I'd been walking but I was back in a familiar place.

People flooded the streets. They seemed to be running to something and running away from something. Traffic made its tune and added to sounds of the city. I recognised this place. I was back in Manhattan.

CHAPTER 13

I entered a public toilet to freshen up. I looked in the mirror and couldn't believe what I saw. I had an overgrown beard and heavy bags under my eyes. My lips were cracked and dry. My face drooped down sadly.

I was far from the angel I knew. I was now just a broken man. I had nowhere to go. Nowhere to be. No love to receive or give. I came out of the public toilet and started crying. People who were passing by took little notice of me and those who did, simply didn't want to get involved.

When my tears had settled down, I looked for a spot where I could just sit and play my guitar. I sat down and placed the guitar case in front of me. I felt hungry and weak, but I knew I had to play something if I was going to get some loose change from anyone. I played for a while and the case started to fill with coins. With my bag of things beside me and my guitar slung across my shoulder, I continued to play, hoping the money could eventually add up to a meal.

CHAPTER 14

I must have dozed off, because I was startled by a tap on my shoulder. I looked up and saw a man in a suit. Somewhere in my mind, I was still playing the guitar. My hands were still holding onto the strings. I looked at him puzzled. The man said to me that a few people off the street had stolen the money in the guitar case and took off. He also said he'd be happy to get me a meal. I looked at the case on the ground and there wasn't any money in it.

'Damn it! I've gotta sing all over again …' I said painfully.

'I'm gonna get myself a hotdog. Can I get you one as well?' asked the man.

I was starving, tired and penniless. I nodded my head as I felt too weak to get up. As the man headed to a nearby hotdog stand, I began to reflect on my life. I had given up everything as an angel only to be living on the streets. I had a music career which I had ruined. My bones felt weak and there was little life left in me. The man came back and handed me a hotdog. I thanked him and took huge bites of my hotdog. He continued to stand around. It looked like he was hoping to speak to me once I was done eating. His phone rang and he said he will speak to me again, but I didn't understand what he meant by that. I was a man who lived off the streets. Why would he want to speak to me? I watched as he hurriedly took off.

I felt my energy lift a little after a couple of minutes. I thought of The One. Why did I leave The One for nothing? All I had was myself and bleak emptiness. I then felt a warm sensation in my heart. I remembered how I had been tasked to help a man in these very streets. Helping that man made me feel so good. Then, I realised that the ground I was sitting on was the very ground I had helped that man almost two years ago. I looked around me. It was exactly the same spot.

I closed my eyes. I asked The One to sincerely change my life around. I didn't want to be in the streets. I asked him to help me. I needed a new start. A sign, a person or anything that could turn my life around. Truth is, from where I was sitting, I didn't have it in me to turn my own life around. Life had beaten me to the ground.

I had realised for a long time I'd stopped loving myself little by little. I wasn't looking after myself. I'd let myself go. I relied heavily on alcohol to get me through my day. I'd lost inspiration to play good music. I cared very little about anyone, and I had certainly given up on love at this point.

My thoughts were getting deeper. What if I had not given up on finding love simply because someone had rejected mine? I felt no love for myself, especially after what had happened with Alice. But what if, I loved myself regardless of my past? I still had the talent to sing and play the guitar. I enjoyed the simple things in life. Even if Alice didn't love me, there would be someone who could. For the first time in my human existence, I realised that loving myself was vital before loving someone else.

I opened my eyes. I remembered the note The One had left me. In all my time of being a human, I had completely forgotten about that note. But today, I remembered – The One would always be there for me. I closed my eyes and made a humble plea to The One. I hoped some miracle would happen. Just at that moment, someone reached out and touched my shoulder.

CHAPTER 15

The suited man from earlier stood above me. I took a closer look at him. He seemed strangely familiar. I was sure I had met him somewhere. I asked him why he had come back to talk to me.

He said about two years ago someone had showed him kindness and he was extending the same to me. He said I wouldn't believe it, but he had been sitting in the same spot as a homeless person just as I was right now. A kind soul had helped him. My eyes welled up. The tears fell from my cheeks not long after. He touched my shoulder once again and said it's okay. He went on to say he knew a shelter that could help me out. He said he would walk me to the shelter if I was interested. I nodded my head in agreement. I knew this was my moment to change my life around. I was going to take it.

After such a long time, it felt good to be human that day. Kindness was shown to me and it felt exhilarating. The word human as I know comes from the Latin word 'humus', meaning earth or ground. I guess we are the very clay of this earth, each and every person, a unique individual. Living a life of kindness and love is what completes us as humans. And when my time expires, I would like to leave this world filled with my kindness and love. I had existed as an angel but would die a human. I gave up being an angel because of love. I will continue my journey to find love now that I have begun to love myself. I will not give up on finding that very feeling that made me want to be human in the first place. I know that I am the first angel to have become human for love. But I have a feeling that I won't be the last. From now on, let it be known that angels can love.

If you enjoyed ANGELS CAN LOVE, check out other books by Victor Paul:

Chapter Thirteen
The Mountain Stole My Wife
Can You See It?

For interested readers,
immerse yourself in the first chapter of:

THE MOUNTAIN STOLE MY WIFE

VICTOR PAUL

CHAPTER 1

2006

Simon

My wife is missing, nowhere to be found. I'm the last person other than the forest ranger to have seen her. The mountain spirit might mean something to the people in this town, but back home in Australia it is absolutely ludicrous. No doubt, I am the main suspect. There is nothing I can do to prove my innocence. My wife is missing and I do not have any answers. She went with me to a sacred spot on the mountain that was forbidden; she has been missing ever since. I came out of the spot alone, desperately looking for my wife. I seemed to be blamed for everything from that point on.

Tony

What do I think of the whole situation? Who knows? Five years with Helen may have caused Simon to push her off the cliff himself. I've known him since high school. There is no way he would hurt anyone, but maybe he reached his limit with her. She controls every aspect of his life. I'm not saying he did it, I'm just saying it's *possible*. I always thought her to be a control freak. Was their relationship as good as it appeared on the outside? I don't know. I asked him what happened on that mountain. All he said was, one minute she was standing on a rock about to take a picture of herself on her phone and the next minute, when he turned around, she was gone. He thought she might be playing a prank or something. But after a few minutes of calling out for her, he realised that she was truly missing. There is this whole thing about this mountain being sacred and people going missing and all. I don't buy it. What happened to her surely has an explanation. I guess the truth will eventually come out. I'm hoping it is not what I think it is. Every man has a breaking point. Did Simon reach his?

Tegan

Simon messaged me and asked if I had heard from Helen. I was confused at first. I thought they were on a holiday together. I got a call from Simon not long after I responded to his message. He told me Helen had been missing for hours. I told him to go to the police immediately, which he had already done. The first thing I thought was, she must have been kidnapped. She is really pretty and wears designer clothes all the time. I'm so scared for her. I really hope she is found soon. You hear all these horror stories in the news about people held captive. I hope none of this is the case and that my best friend returns to the motel they are staying at. This is certainly not how their wedding anniversary holiday should have started. I feel terrible for them.

Richard

Simon is responsible for my daughter's disappearance. I have no doubt about that. Why would my son-in-law call me almost two days later to say that Helen is missing? Two days! Was he buying time to cover up his act and come up with a story? I think he's behind all of this. I'm going to get to the bottom of the matter. I've been in the police force for years—something is not right here.